Published by Grolier Enterprises Corp.,
Danbury, Connecticut

ISBN: 7172-8192-2

A DISNEY RHYMING READER

PINOCCHIO AND THE MAGIC CLOCK

Fun with Words About the Seasons

A DISNEY RHYMING READER

PINOCCHIO AND THE MAGIC CLOCK

Grolier Enterprises Corp.

"Pinocchio, look at my clock.
It does much more than go ticktock,"
Geppetto said. "This clock's so smart,
It shows the seasons as they start."

"In winter you can see the snow.
In spring birds sing and flowers grow.
In summer the hot sun shines down.
In fall the leaves turn red and brown."

The Blue Fairy appeared that night.
She waved her wand. The clock grew bright.
She said, "The season this clock shows
Will be the season the world knows."

The next day Geppetto declared,
"Our clock's so nice, it should be shared.
Take it to the mayor, my boy.
This gift will bring our town great joy."

Pinocchio looked at the time
While two thieves planned their latest crime.
Foulfellow the fox was quite bold.
Gideon did as he was told.

Foulfellow said, "That clock is great,
And here's how we can get it, mate.
He's just a kid, easy to trick.
I'll talk to him. You grab it quick!"

"Excuse me, sir," the sly fox cried.
"I think I'm lost. I need a guide.
Could you tell me the best way to
A far-off land called Timbuktu?"

"I'm sorry," said Pinocchio.
"That place is one that I don't know."
Meanwhile, Gideon sneaked behind.
He had a single thought in mind.

His paws reached out. He grabbed the prize.
Pinocchio watched him in surprise.
Then down the hill ran Gideon.
It looked as if the thieves had won.

Pinocchio shouted, "Come back here!"
The thief kept running like a deer.
"Stop!" said the boy. "You can't take that!"
Then he began to chase the cat.

The cat was leading in this race,
Until he fell flat on his face.
He did not see a great big rock,
And when he tripped, he dropped the clock.

The clock banged hard against the ground.
The hands spun crazily around.
Then the Blue Fairy's spell took hold.
The weather changed from hot to cold!

Winter snow turned the landscape white.
Gideon felt the cold wind's bite.
There were icicles on the trees.
Gideon's nose began to freeze.

A snowstorm at this time of year!
The cat thought, "Something's crazy here!"
The puzzled cat was still in shock
When Pinocchio grabbed the clock.

He ran away. Now it was spring!
He heard a nest of robins sing.
There were green buds on all the trees,
And daffodils swayed in the breeze.

But Pinocchio did not see
Foulfellow hiding near a tree.
The fox tripped him as he went by.
He lost the clock. That fox was sly!

Pinocchio took up the chase.
A summer sun now warmed his face.
Bees and butterflies were in flight.
The mean fox was nowhere in sight.

Pinocchio climbed up a hill.
"I'll get that fox. I know I will.
For Geppetto's sake, I can't fail."
But he had lost Foulfellow's trail.

The season changed. Now it was fall.
Harvests were in. Corn stalks stood tall.
There were pumpkins and falling leaves.
He said, "Why can't I find those thieves?"

And then the weather changed once more.
Up ahead it began to pour.
"This wind is like a hurricane.
I bet our clock has caused this rain."

He ran and found his guess was right.
The villains were a sorry sight.
"Help," said the fox. "I can't swim."
Pinocchio just looked at him.

The water rose up to their necks.
They looked a lot like two shipwrecks.
The clock made so much rain come down,
The two thieves floated out of town.

He picked the clock up just in time.
He saw it was about to chime.
He turned it off because he feared
The weather would become too weird.

Quickly the weather turned just right.
The clock was off. The sun shone bright.
"Hurray," Pinocchio shouted then.
"We have normal seasons again!"

Pinocchio came running back.
"This clock's a mess. It's out of whack.
But Geppetto will fix it fast—
Then we can give our gift at last."

The people of the town were glad
To honor the heroic lad.
Geppetto, too, was in the throng.
The happy crowd clapped loud and long.

The mayor said, "Because of you,
Pinocchio, those thieves are through.
The clock is safe. We'll keep it here.
And now let's give this boy a cheer!"

How Many of These Words About the Seasons Do You Know?

WINTER

Snow

Snowstorm

Icicles

SPRING

Buds

Daffodils

Robins

Nest

SUMMER

Butterflies

Sun

Bees

FALL

Pumpkins

Harvest

Falling Leaves

Wind